THE SPELL OF CHUCHUCHAN

THE SPELL OF
CHUCHUCHAN

Elfreida Read

Illustrated by Betty Fraser

THE WORLD PUBLISHING COMPANY

CLEVELAND AND NEW YORK

Published by The World Publishing Company
2231 West 110th Street, Cleveland, Ohio 44102
First American Edition 1967
Library of Congress catalog card number: 67-23345
PP
Text copyright © 1966 by Elfreida Read
Illustrations copyright © 1967 by Betty Fraser
Designed by Jack Jaget

CONTENTS

THE SPELL OF CHUCHUCHAN

THE WEDDING

IN A LITTLE village in China, very long ago, lived a little girl called Kei-lin. All around the village stretched green rice fields, and although Kei-lin loved the fields and the home where she lived with her aunt and uncle, she always longed for something new, for some adventure.

So when she heard that a very dear cousin of hers was going to get married in the faraway town of Senfu, Kei-lin begged her aunt to let her go to the wedding.

"Well," said her aunt, "we really had no intention of taking you, or Mei-dee." Mei-dee was the aunt's own daughter, and she and Kei-lin were like sisters, for Kei-lin had come to live with her aunt when she was a tiny baby and her parents had died.

"Oh, Auntie, please take us with you," Kei-lin begged, her black eyes shining, while Mei-dee stood by looking a little anxious, for she was not as bold as Kei-lin. "We will be good," Kei-lin promised, "and we will help with all the preparations. Oh,

9

Auntie, how can you think of leaving us at home when we both love Linza so much."

And indeed this was true. Linza had visited them and both Mei-dee and Kei-lin had fallen in love with her. She was very beautiful with large, almond-shaped eyes, and a sweet smile. She had made clothes for their dolls, and shown them a new way to fly their kites. And now Linza, the most beautiful girl in the whole province, was going to be married.

"Well," said her aunt again, "well, we shall see." But by the way she said it, Kei-lin knew that she would take them, and she flung her arms around the kind woman's neck and hugged her so tight that her long black hair came tumbling down.

Soon came that most delightful of all jobs, packing for the trip.

"What are you going to take with you, Kei-lin?" asked Mei-dee.

"I'm going to take my slippers with the butterflies on them, and my little statue of the Goddess of Mercy, and of course all the new clothes Auntie got me. Oh Mei-dee, we'll see so many new people and places and all sorts of things. Oh, we'll have fun!"

"And I'll take my little doll and my carved box—I know, I can put her clothes in the box—oh, I'll make her a new set of clothes for the wedding too." Mei-dee's face beamed with happiness at the thought.

So it was that in a little time Kei-lin and Mei-dee

found themselves traveling to the town of Senfu. First they traveled in an oxcart with their little red boxes at their feet. Then they traveled on a large junk and finally in sedan chairs for many, many days. There were many stopping places on the way where the carriers of the chairs were changed, and Kei-lin became tired and bored with the endless journey, but of course she dared not grumble because it had been her idea to come—and there was Senfu and Linza's wedding at the end of the journey.

And indeed Kei-lin was not disappointed. They reached Senfu safely. It was a dear little town, deep in the heart of the mountains. Kei-lin was excited at seeing Linza again. Linza herself was deeply happy for she was marrying a young and handsome man. Of course the marriage had been planned by Linza's parents and the parents of the young man, for that was the custom in China, but Linza had long known this young man, and had long been secretly in love with him.

Kei-lin rode in the wedding procession in a sedan chair together with all the most important relatives, and later, at the wedding feast, she sat next to Linza. She was so happy she could scarcely eat anything at all. Linza, too, did not eat very much. She looked so lovely in her red gown with a flower just behind her small white ear.

And then a curious thing happened. One of the servants brought a gift to the bride. He said a stranger had left it at the gate and had then hurried

away. It was wrapped in the special bright red paper used for gifts, and sealed with a strange gold seal. Linza unwrapped the gift. Inside was a box. Linza opened the lid. Within the box lay a single yellow flower.

Kei-lin saw Linza flush and then turn very white. She passed the box to her mother, who clapped her hand to her mouth to stop the scream that rose in her throat. Kei-lin then remembered that the yellow flower had always been a sign of bad luck in their family.

"Who could have sent that?" cried Linza's mother. "Call the servants. Catch the evil-doer." Linza's father hastened to calm her mother and the guests at the feast, all of whom were upset. "The person probably did not know that the yellow flower is a sign of bad luck in our family. He only meant to please you," he said. Nonetheless the servants were sent out. But the street was empty by then, the stranger gone.

"It doesn't matter," said Linza's father soothingly. "Calm yourselves. We will give the flower to the priest at the temple and he will pray to the gods and charm the evil out of it. Stop worrying everyone, and have another glass of wine."

And so the flower was sent away to the temple and the guests returned to the feast.

"Kei-lin," Linza said later on when the excitement was over. "I have an idea. Why don't you ask Auntie to let you stay here for a while? Just to visit. Perhaps a month or two. And then we will send you home with Ah-Mo. You will be perfectly safe."

"Oh, Linza, how I'd love to," Kei-lin whispered, scarcely believing her good luck. Ah-Mo was a loyal and trusted servant of the whole family, really almost a family member, and when Kei-lin's aunt heard the proposal, she had very little objection. Linza asked Mei-dee too, but Mei-dee was different from Kei-lin. She wanted to go back home with her mother.

So when the wedding was over Kei-lin's aunt and uncle and Mei-dee left the town of Senfu, and Kei-lin remained at the home of Linza's new husband. The family was large and the home consisted of many houses joined by courtyards, and it wasn't long before Kei-lin got to know everyone in the family and was welcome in every house. Linza took her to the theater, where the actors danced and sang, and she took her to Punch and Judy shows where Kei-lin laughed and laughed and couldn't stop laughing. Only one thing happened to spoil Kei-lin's stay with Linza.

It happened upon a sunny day when Kei-lin was playing in one of the many courtyards of Linza's home. Two old ladies were sitting on a bench quite close to her under a spreading peach tree, and they were talking.

"Nothing has happened to Linza so far," said one of them, "but I am worried."

"I am worried too," said the other. "That yellow flower has always brought bad luck to our family. Even though Linza's father took it to the temple, Linza did touch it first."

"It seems to me that it was sent as a token—almost as if the sender was warning us to expect the worst,"said the first.

"Linza is such a beautiful girl," said the second. "There are always wicked gods and spirits who are waiting for a chance to steal away our beautiful girls."

Kei-lin sat very still on the floor of the courtyard and little chills of fear went through her. For many days she worried about what the two old ladies had said, but as the days went by and nobody stole Linza away, and nothing dreadful happened, she stopped worrying and began to enjoy her visit again, soon forgetting all about the matter.

The time passed by very quickly, and at last the day came to say good-bye.

"You'll come again, dear little Kei-lin," whispered Linza, hugging her with tears in her great brown eyes. "You'll come again very soon. We will all miss you. Look, here's something very special for you." She put a small box into Kei-lin's hand. "Open it, and see if you like it."

Kei-lin opened the box and in it lay the loveliest bracelet she had ever seen. It was made of filigree silver and set with glowing red stones. Kei-lin caught her breath with delight.

"Isn't it lovely?" Linza said, who was delighted with the bracelet herself. "And besides, it's a charm. It will keep you safe. Put it on your arm, and don't you ever take it off." Kei-lin put the bracelet on, and Linza kissed her good-bye.

And there was the sedan chair waiting for her, a fine chair with bright hangings and little windows with curtains through which Kei-lin could peep if she wanted to, and her chest was hoisted up and placed at her feet. Another sedan chair was ready behind her for Ah-Mo. So with much waving and many promises to return, Kei-lin was carried down the street by the four bearers on her way back to her aunt and uncle and little Mei-dee.

THE STORM

THIS TIME the journey seemed much longer. Of course there was nothing exciting at the end of it, only home and Kei-lin's uncle and aunt and Mei-dee. Kei-lin sighed with impatience as the sedan chair bobbed up and down along the endless, uneven road. She did not even have anyone to talk to.

"I suppose I shouldn't be so greedy," she thought to herself, "I've had so much fun during the last month or two. But I do wish something interesting would happen." But the sedan chair went on and on, stopping only for food and changing carriers. Ah-Mo would come out of his chair and stretch and yawn and talk to Kei-lin for a bit, and then he would go to the little hut by the side of the road where the carriers lived, and where the food was sold, and buy her something special that she liked. He was very kind and very generous, but not very exciting.

At last they reached the seashore and boarded

the junk which was to take them on the next stage of their journey. Kei-lin liked to sail in the junk and her spirits revived a little. She hurried onto its wooden decks and examined once again the huge sails which the sailors were so clever at hoisting up and lowering again. She wished she could do that too, but Ah-Mo would not let her talk to any of the sailors and told her to sit down quietly on a little seat in the stern of the boat. Soon the junk cast off and started on its journey south.

Kei-lin enjoyed watching the water swirling behind the junk and the sea rolling to the horizon, tossing and churning, and now lifting and now dropping the little vessel on its restless back. This was better than that dusty road and the endless paddy fields. When it became dark Ah-Mo took her below and showed her a place where she could sleep. It was only a narrow bunk bed, but Kei-lin was very tired and fell asleep quickly. And so day by day the junk sped on, carried by its huge brown sails, and the few days of journeying by sea were nearly over.

One morning Kei-lin slept a little late, and when she came out on deck she found the weather had changed. Instead of an endless blue expanse all around her and clear skies, she found angry gray waters and a sky covered with clouds. The junk was heaving far more than it had been during the days past, and Kei-lin felt a little frightened.

"There's a storm coming up," said Ah-Mo, "but don't be frightened. This is a good strong junk and it has weathered many storms."

About noon the wind started to rise and the waves became very big. Kei-lin was told by Ah-Mo to go below deck and she went, but she became more frightened, and as the little vessel rolled and heaved she clung to her bunk and prayed to the Goddess of Mercy to take care of her. She remembered Linza's bracelet too, and made sure it was safely on her arm; then she felt a little better. But the storm did not get any less, and when Ah-Mo brought her a bowl of tea in the early afternoon she saw that he looked frightened too.

In the late afternoon the storm became worse than ever. The junk rolled in a terrifying way and Kei-lin had to hang onto her bunk to prevent herself from being hurled against the opposite wall. Water streamed in from the deck and covered the floor of the little room. She could hear the sailors shouting at one another and there was a great deal of running on the deck above. She wanted to climb out of her bunk and run up to the deck to see what was happening, but when she looked down she could see that the water on the floor had risen several inches.

She began to feel trapped in the little room, and tears rose to her eyes. She was just going to call to Ah-Mo when suddenly there was a resounding crash and a sound of great planks of wood splintering. Kei-lin jumped down into the water on the floor and climbed up the narrow steps to the deck, where a dreadful sight met her eyes.

The junk had split nearly in half and was stuck high up on a rock. The sailors had all clambered onto the half that was out of the water and only Kei-lin was left on the half that was sinking. She started to shriek for help when her half of the vessel collapsed and she found herself struggling in the water.

"Help," she shouted feebly, for all her breath had been knocked out by the coldness of the water, "help, help," but of course none of the sailors heard her, or even saw her, for the storm had made the day very dark and the waves were so wild.

Kei-lin was just beginning to sink when suddenly she felt an iron-like grip around her body and in the next instant she was lifted right out of the waves and was flying high above the sea. She couldn't understand what had happened—her head was spinning and her ears were ringing—but in a few moments she found herself deposited in a dry spot under a great overhanging rock, well out of the way of the storm. She looked up to see who her rescuer was and could scarcely believe her eyes when she saw that it was a huge green dragon!

"Why, it's you!" cried Kei-lin breathlessly.

"Yes," agreed the dragon, "and a lucky thing for you too. And now I have to go and look for my tail which I've lost in the sea. Don't you move out of this spot now."

Of course Kei-lin had no intention of moving anywhere.

Huge and fierce and thousands of years old, nonetheless the dragon was Kei-lin's very best friend. They had been through many adventures

together, and Kei-lin knew that whenever the dragon appeared something exciting usually followed. She could scarcely wait for him to get back, but at last he did, dragging his long, clumsy tail.

"Hitch it on for me, will you Kei-lin?" he said. "You know I can't do a thing without it. It was lucky the waves washed it up on shore. Otherwise I'd have had to set all the sea gods looking for it. But here it is—wet, but safe and sound."

Kei-lin was beginning to feel a little more like her old self, although she was wet and cold. "Haven't you done anything about that tail of yours yet?" she asked. "You know, you'll lose it for good one day and then what will you do?"

"I don't know," said the dragon, "I really must attend to it. But hurry now. I'm going to build you a fire here in this sheltered spot."

So Kei-lin lifted the tail carefully to where the scales fitted over it and it clicked safely into place.

"Now," said the dragon, "I shall make you a fire."

"But what about all the sailors," cried Kei-lin, "and Ah-Mo? You must save them too."

"They are all safe," the dragon told her. "The junk broke in half just by the shore and spilled them all out on the reef, and the villagers from the cottages on the cliffs are out there rescuing them. There is no need for me. In fact half of them would probably die of fright if they saw me."

"There's something in that," Kei-lin said. She was even beginning to be able to laugh again. She remembered Linza's bracelet and was relieved to find it still clasped on her arm. The dragon soon had a roaring fire going. Kei-lin dried her clothes and herself and felt better and better, but she was hungry and there was nothing to eat.

"Wait a minute," said the dragon, "I'll get you something to eat."

He lumbered out of the sheltered spot and Kei-lin lost sight of him in the wind and rain. "Oh dear," she thought anxiously, "I do hope nothing happens to him." But she need not have worried, for in a short while he came back, dripping wet, but carrying two squirming fish in his mouth.

"How did you ever get those?" cried Kei-lin.

The dragon did not answer her, only grinned his remarkable grin, and pretty soon Kei-lin had a delicious dinner of fried fish.

In the meantime the storm had begun to abate. The dragon looked out of their shelter.

"It's still windy," he said, "but the rain is stopping. We should be able to start back to your village pretty soon."

"What shall I do about Ah-Mo?" Kei-lin asked. "He will be in the village on the cliffs breaking his heart, thinking that I drowned."

"We'll leave a message for him," said the dragon. "We'll tell him not to worry—that you will be home long before he will." And this was true, for the junk had been blown far out of its course and it would be many, many days before Ah-Mo could find his way back to Kei-lin's village. And of course the old man would never think of agreeing to fly on the back of a dragon!

So the dragon carried Kei-lin to the outskirts of the village and Kei-lin left a message for Ah-Mo. Then she climbed onto the dragon's back and he rose into the air, at first slowly and then with gathering speed, until Kei-lin could feel the wind whistling past her ears and her pigtail standing straight out behind her. It was not a new feeling, for Kei-lin had been on the dragon's back many times in the past and it was very thrilling indeed.

They had been flying for quite a while and the sun had set and the skies had darkened when Kei-lin noticed a strange light ahead of them. It did not look like an ordinary star and she called the dragon's attention to it. He gave a pleased chortle.

"Why, it's the Goddess of the Northern Star," he cried. "We haven't seen her for a long time. Let's speak to her. She always has something interesting to say." And he streaked through the heavens in the direction of the curious light.

As they came closer the bright light turned into the shape of a very odd goddess indeed. Kei-lin was not surprised, for she had seen her before, but she simply could not get used to her. The Goddess of the Northern Star had three eyes and eighteen arms, and she moved through the air seated on a lotus throne.

She had explained this to Kei-lin before. She had so many children—all the stars in the heaven were her children—that she had had to grow extra arms to cope with them all. She had grown an extra eye, too, so that it could keep watch over the heavens while her two ordinary ones were sleeping. And she was seated on a throne because she was Empress of the Heavens and Queen of the Night.

"How wonderful to see you two again," she cried as they came nearer. "Oh, there's all sorts of gossip I'm just dying to tell you. Did you hear that the Kitchen God got cross with the Heavenly Dog again and held up his order of bones, so of course the Dog started to snap at the moon—and naturally *I* had to be called in to smooth over the quarrel—oh, it was the funniest thing." And the merry goddess laughed so loudly that the heavens rang with her mirth.

Kei-lin laughed too, so heartily that she nearly slipped off the dragon's back and had to hang on to his scales. "Oh tell us some more," she cried.

"Well, the main thing I have to tell you about," said the goddess, weaving her many arms gently through the air and rocking a little on her lotus throne, "isn't at all funny. It is very sad indeed, and we are all trying to think of something to do about it. Have you ever heard of Chuchuchan?"

"Chuchuchan?" the dragon repeated. "I should say I have. He is a very unpleasant creature indeed." And itching with curiosity, Kei-lin cried, "Who is he? Tell me."

"Chuchuchan," said the Goddess of the Northern Star to Kei-lin, "is a very evil god. I would say he is the very worst god that I know of."

"Well, what has he done?" asked the dragon.

"He has bewitched a whole city," said the Goddess of the Northern Star. "It is lying in a deep sleep. And he has stolen the most beautiful maiden in the whole of the city's province and taken her to his castle in the Kun Lun mountains. She was only recently married to a handsome young man and now this dreadful thing has happened. No one can approach the city, for as soon as they enter the ring of enchantment, they fall asleep. We are all racking our brains to see what we can do."

"That's really a dreadful thing," the dragon agreed shaking his head. "I shall have to try to help you too, as soon as I get Kei-lin safely home."

"It all started at the wedding feast," went on the Goddess of the Northern Star. "Everything had been going so well, when someone brought a gift to the bride. The gift was a sign of bad luck to the whole family. It was a yellow flower—"

Kei-lin gave a horrified shriek. "A yellow flower!" she cried, and her limbs became so weak that she could scarcely hold on to the dragon's scales.

"Yes, a yellow flower," the goddess repeated. "Why, child, what is the matter with you? You look quite ill."

"What was the name of the town . . . the name of the girl . . ." Kei-lin cried. "Tell me, who was it?"

"It is the little town of Senfu," said the Goddess of the Northern Star, "deep in the heart of the western mountains. And the name of the girl was Linza."

THE PALACE OF THE
GREAT BEAR

KEI-LIN had the greatest difficulty holding on to the dragon's scales.

"Take care, child," said the Goddess of the Northern Star. "Do you know how many thousands of feet you are above the earth? You can't go slithering around like that."

"But do you know what you just said!" gasped Kei-lin. "The girl you just mentioned—she is my cousin—the cousin I love best in the world—I was at her wedding two months ago—don't you see?"

The goddess steadied Kei-lin with one of her numerous arms.

"That's a terrible thing," she cried, and the dragon twisted his neck around to look at Kei-lin.

"We have to save her," cried Kei-lin. "At once. There isn't a moment to lose."

"Wait a moment," said the Goddess of the Northern Star. "Of course we must save her. But it isn't as easy as all that. For one thing we are dealing with one of the most powerful gods in China. He is much more powerful than I am, for instance, or the dragon there. We have to find a way to outwit him somehow."

"You may not be so powerful," said Kei-lin, "but you're clever. You must think of something."

"But Kei-lin," the dragon put in, "you're supposed to be going home. How can you set out on adventures now to save your cousin?"

"Nothing is more important than Linza," Kei-lin said. "I would do anything to help her."

"Let me see," said the goddess thoughtfully, swaying on her throne and folding her eighteen arms gently around her. She closed two of her eyes and the third one gazed far away into space. "Now the thing to do is to find someone who would know how to break Chuchuchan's spell. Who would that someone be?" She remained silent for a while longer, while the dragon floated almost motionless in the air and Kei-lin fidgeted on his back. "I know," exclaimed the goddess suddenly. "Of course, the very person!"

"Who? Who?" cried Kei-lin impatiently. "Oh tell us quickly."

"Wen Chang, the God of Literature," said the goddess triumphantly. "Do you know, the creature has read every single piece of writing in the whole world. He knows everything. So of course he would be the person to ask. He would know what we'd have to do to break the spell of Chuchuchan."

"Where would we find him?" asked Kei-lin.

"His palace is in the Great Bear," replied the

goddess. "He lives with his two servants who are called 'Heaven-deaf' and 'Earth-mute.' One is deaf and the other cannot speak, and so in this way the God of Literature keeps all his secrets. One servant cannot hear any of his secrets and the other, although he may hear them, cannot pass them on."

"How clever," Kei-lin said, "but in that case they won't be of much use to us."

"No," said the goddess, "but they are kind-hearted things and they might try to help you. I have to warn you that the God of Literature is by no means the sweet gentleman you might expect him to be. He is quite difficult and is not always willing to grant people their requests. So you have a problem on your hands. But try anyway. If you don't succeed, we'll have to do something else, although I can't think what."

"I'm sure we'll succeed somehow," Kei-lin said. "We just have to. We can't leave Linza in the hands of such an evil god. And think of all those lovely people I got to know in Senfu—all bewitched. Oh, we just have to succeed."

"Do you think you'll find your way to the Great Bear?" asked the goddess of the dragon.

"Oh, yes," said the dragon. "It is a fine, clear night, and the Great Bear is perfectly visible. We won't have any trouble, I'm sure. Thank you for your suggestions."

"Good luck to you," said the goddess. "I'm sorry I can't come with you. I'm so busy, I really can't spare the time. But I shall be waiting to hear your news, and I'll keep my third eye on you. Good-bye." And as Kei-lin and the dragon said good-bye to her she began to move away from them, waving her eighteen arms.

"I hope the enchantment won't be too hard to break," Kei-lin thought as she sat on the dragon's back. The flight took them the rest of the night, and in the morning they arrived in a barren country and saw a palace perched on a craggy hill.

"I suppose that is Wen Chang's palace," Kei-lin said. "Let's go and find out." So the dragon flew to the courtyard which surrounded the palace and alighted on the flags. There was absolute stillness around them.

"I'll go to the door," said Kei-lin, "but you stay close behind me. It's eerie here."

"Very well," said the dragon. Kei-lin ventured slowly up the high stone steps to the front door of the palace. The stone steps were cracked and un-even underfoot, and the whole front of the palace looked in need of a good new coat of paint. It was very shabby. "Maybe he's too busy learning all the time," Kei-lin thought, "or maybe he's not very rich." There was a large brass knocker on the door and after hesitating for a few moments Kei-lin lifted it and gave a gentle rap.

For a while nothing happened. As soon as the sound of the rap died away the silence descended again. Kei-lin waited for a few moments, glancing back at the dragon. Then when she was just stretch-ing out her hand to knock again the door opened inward, slowly and soundlessly.

Two little men in identical clothes, with little mandarin caps on their heads, stood before Kei-lin. They bowed. Kei-lin bowed too. They waited politely with their hands tucked inside their wide sleeves.

"Please," said Kei-lin, "I would like to speak to Wen Chang."

"What did she say?" asked the deaf one of the mute. The mute made a sign with his hands, and then they both stood aside to allow Kei-lin to enter.

The hall was long and gloomy. Kei-lin looked back at the dragon, but realized that he was far too large to enter with her. She would have to go on her own. The little men shut the door after her, which made the hall darker than ever. Kei-lin shivered inside her little blue jacket. The servants padded along ahead of her, and she knew she had to follow them. They led her to the very end of the hall where there was a tall paneled doorway. Pushing aside one of the panels, they gestured to her to enter. Kei-lin did so and then wished she hadn't, for the door behind her slid shut and she was left to face the god alone.

She looked around the room. Wherever she looked there were shelves with scrolls and tablets and bamboo sheets, all holding the writings of many centuries past and all dusty and in need of a good spring cleaning. "Except I expect he'd never let the servants do it for then they might learn some of his secrets," she thought. The far end of the room was lit by an oil lamp which was set on a very large table, and a figure sat at the table with his back to her—a huge figure, so huge that Kei-lin shook in her shoes just to see him.

As her eyes became used to the gloom she could see that the table was covered from end to end with silk and bamboo scrolls, all higgledy-piggledy, and some had even spilled over onto the floor.

Kei-lin wished Heaven-deaf and Earth-mute had not left her alone. However there was nothing for it but to make her presence known to the god.

"Excuse me," said Kei-lin in a tiny voice. There was no answer, so she tried a little louder. "Excuse me." There was still no answer, so Kei-lin walked, her legs feeling very shaky, across the large room to the god at the table. When she was standing almost beside him, she said again, "Excuse me."

This time he heard her and swung around. He had a long beard which was carefully separated into three parts, and long mustachios, so long that they reached and mingled with the beard. He towered over her even when he was sitting.

"Who are you?" he asked crossly. "You know story characters are never allowed to come alive until the sun has set. It's only just morning."

"I am Kei-lin," said Kei-lin stoutly. "I am not a story character. I have come to visit you. I am a little girl from the earth."

"You should know that only authors and story characters are allowed to visit me," said the god.

"But I have a very important reason for visiting you," Kei-lin insisted. "I came with the dragon. You know him."

"I know him well enough," said the god. "The last of the dragons. But even he had no business bringing you."

"But I'm very anxious to ask you something," Kei-lin begged.

The god sighed, crossed his arms on the table, and put his head on them. "Well, what is it?" he asked.

"You have read all the books in the world," said Kei-lin, "and have studied everything under the sun. Could you tell us how to break one of Chuchuchan's spells?"

"Chuchuchan!" exclaimed the god, springing upright. "You would meddle with Chuchuchan! You must have lost your mind, child."

"No, no, I haven't," Kei-lin cried. "You see, Chuchuchan has bewitched the dearest person in the world and I simply have to find some way to save her. He has stolen my cousin Linza from the town of Senfu and has put the town to sleep. We simply have to find a way to break his spell."

"You expect me to interfere with Chuchuchan?"

"I didn't think you'd be afraid," Kei-lin said artfully.

The god bristled. His mustachios even stood up a little. "Who's afraid?" he growled. "I'm not afraid of anything. But I don't care about anything either. Why should I care if your cousin has been stolen? Why should I care if the town of Senfu has been put to sleep? Why should I care about these things? Tell me that."

Kei-lin didn't know how to answer him. "But of course you should care," she said at last. "How can you not care when someone else is miserable?"

"Listen, child. I am the God of Literature, and I've been sitting here for hundreds of years reading every single thought that has ever come out of anyone with a brain. I've read everything and I know everything. And do you think I'm happy? No! I am the most miserable god in the universe."

"But why?" Kei-lin stammered. "I can't understand you."

"No, you can't understand me. Why should you? You don't know what it's like to look for happiness for hundreds of years and never find it. Do you know that I've looked for happiness in every scroll, on every writing tablet that has ever come my way, and I've found nothing. I've searched and searched and searched, only for happiness, and I'm miserable, miserable, miserable!" His voice rose on every word and on the last one he smote his fists against the table and several more scrolls fell to the floor.

Kei-lin felt she couldn't say anything at all. She stood very quietly.

"So you see I don't care if the whole world is miserable. I don't care if all your cousins get stolen. I don't care if Chuchuchan puts the whole silly earth to sleep. If I can't find happiness for myself, why should I help anyone else find it?"

Once more Kei-lin had no answer.

"Go away, little girl. Go away from here. Find some way to make me happy and I will find a way to save your cousin and to break the spell of Chuchuchan. Now go, go. I have work to do. Look at all these new writings. Perhaps somewhere among them I shall find happiness. Away, little girl."

HEAVEN-DEAF AND EARTH-MUTE TAKE A HAND

SOFTLY Kei-lin crossed the room, noiselessly slid open the panel and stepped into the hall. She was immediately met by Heaven-deaf and Earth-mute. They looked so friendly that Kei-lin felt tears rise to her eyes and one by one roll down her cheeks. Heaven-deaf handed her a handkerchief, while Earth-mute took her arm and led her into another room off the hall. It was small and very shabbily furnished, as was everything in the palace. There was a little rosewood table in the middle of the room, scratched and worn from long use, and some benches around it. Earth-mute led her to one of the benches and signed for her to sit down. Then he went to a dresser at the side and brought a pot of tea and some bowls. Heaven-deaf sat down with Kei-lin.

"You must know first of all," he said, "that we are not allowed to speak to strangers. Not at all. But we feel very sorry for you, so we are taking the chance. If Wen Chang finds out that we have been talking to you, he will be very angry."

"The Goddess of the Northern Star told us," Kei-lin said, "that Wen Chang took you as servants because one of you was deaf and the other mute, so that his secrets would never be revealed." Heaven-deaf looked at Earth-mute, who quickly translated what Kei-lin said in sign language.

"That is so," said Heaven-deaf. "However, we have been here for so long that we have learned to understand each other, even though Wen Chang does not know this. We know a great deal more of his business than he thinks. Tell us what you want of him, for we might be able to help you."

Quickly Kei-lin told her story and then said, "I only asked him to tell us how to break Chuchu-chan's spell, and he became quite angry. He said he didn't care if other people were unhappy."

"It is true. Wen Chang really doesn't care about anyone. He is very unhappy himself, and when persons are unhappy they don't care about anyone else. He has been searching for happiness for hundreds and hundreds of years and he can't find it. He has all the knowledge in the world and it doesn't make him happy."

"But what shall I do?" Kei-lin sighed. She sipped the hot tea and it comforted her a little, but her heart was very heavy.

Heaven-deaf and Earth-mute moved away to the other end of the little room and talked, Heaven-deaf in a low voice, Earth-mute in his sign language, and then they came back to the table.

"We have decided to help you," said Heaven-deaf. "We feel that what you are doing is very important, and we cannot let Wen Chang's bad mood interfere. Tonight, when Wen Chang is fast asleep, we will go to the rooms where he keeps all the writings in the world and we will search for those which will tell us how to break the spells of Chuchuchan. In the meantime you will have to go back to your dragon and pretend to fly away. Then at midnight you must return, and we will do our best. Be very quiet indeed when you return. We will be waiting for you at the door. Do not knock or make a single sound, or things will go badly. And now you had better go before Wen Chang discovers us."

Hastily Kei-lin left the mysterious palace of the God of Literature and found the dragon in the courtyard. "Come on," she said, "I'll tell you everything as we go."

"Where are we going?" asked the dragon.

"Just away," replied Kei-lin. "Somewhere out of sight of the palace. Quite far away."

"Well, don't keep me in suspense," the dragon said as they flew away from the palace. "What happened?" Shouting against the wind, Kei-lin told him everything.

"I always knew Wen Chang was a bad-tempered old fellow, but I didn't think he was getting as bad as that," the dragon called back. "I hope Heaven-deaf and Earth-mute know what they are about, otherwise they can get into a lot of trouble."

"Look," said Kei-lin, "there's a nice grassy place

down below, and some trees with fruit. Let's stop here and wait. Maybe we can eat the fruit."

So they descended to the grassy knoll, and found the fruit on the trees very nice to eat. Then, since they were both tired, they lay down and slept soundly.

When Kei-lin woke up it was very dark and very quiet. The dragon was snoring gently beside her. It seemed a pity to wake him, but as she had no idea what time it was there was nothing else to do. She shook him gently. He snorted and awoke.

"Have you any idea what time it is?" she asked anxiously. "You know I have to be at the palace at midnight." The dragon shook his head vigorously to get all the sleep out of it. "Do we really have to go already? I feel so sleepy," he said.

"Yes, we do," said Kei-lin.

They flew back to the palace and when Kei-lin tiptoed up the big steps the two tiny men appeared at once and signed to her to be very quiet. The dragon lay down in the courtyard, put his head on his paws, and fell fast asleep again.

Kei-lin followed Heaven-deaf and Earth-mute into the palace. If it was gloomy and mysterious in the daytime—it was ten times worse at night. A very dim oil lamp was burning in the great entrance hall, and Heaven-deaf took it off the wall to light their way up some stairs at the side of the hall. "Look where you're going," he whispered to Kei-lin; "we have to be very quiet."

Kei-lin stepped carefully up the stairs and they

soon found themselves in what looked like another hall, with many doors leading off it. Earth-mute led them across to a door at the far end. He opened it very carefully and they all three entered.

The room was full of shelves and cupboards and tables, and everything was filled and covered with writings. There were writings on wooden tablets and on porcelain tablets, there were writings carefully rolled in scrolls, and writings on silk and bamboo sheets. There were hundreds of writings, and Kei-lin's heart sank, for she felt it would be impossible to find what they were looking for among so many words.

Heaven-deaf and Earth-mute signed to her to sit down at a table in the very middle of the room, and they sat down on either side of her. In the middle of the table there was a fine incense holder and Earth-mute lit a taper at the oil lamp they had brought with them and ignited the incense. As soon as the faint perfume rose into the air Earth-mute made some slow movements with his hands while Heaven-deaf chanted in a soft singsong voice:

> "Light aglow
> Magic flow,
> Lan Tan Tin
> Enter in."

and as Kei-lin peered through the gloom, she suddenly saw by the dim light of the oil lamp that a fourth figure had joined them at the table.

She knew right away that this was a spirit, but as

Kei-lin was used to unusual persons like dragons and gods and even demons, she felt more curious than frightened.

"Lan Tan Tin," said Heaven-deaf, "we have a great favor to ask of you."

"What is it?" asked the spirit.

"Somewhere here in this great house, full of all the writings in the world, is something you once wrote about the spells of Chuchuchan."

"Yes, there is," agreed Lan Tan Tin.

"Chuchuchan has just laid one of his spells over a whole city and stolen a beautiful girl, whom he is keeping a prisoner in his castle, and we want to find out how to break his spell. But there are so many writings here that we would never find what we are looking for. Can you help us?"

"Yes," said Lan Tan Tin. He had a little beard and a black cap on his head. "My writings about Chuchuchan are kept in a very secret vault at the other end of the palace. You can imagine that anything like magic or spells would have to be guarded extra carefully in case it is stolen. Follow me, and I will show you exactly where my writings are kept."

Once more Kei-lin found herself in the gloomy hall, tiptoeing after Heaven-deaf and Earth-mute, who in turn tiptoed after the spirit of Lan Tan Tin. He was the only one who did not tiptoe, for he wafted gently across the hall like a leaf blown by the wind. He led them to the other end of the palace and they entered a room that looked much like the one they had left, except that one wall had no shelves or cupboards, but only a row of panels. Lan Tan Tin flitted to the paneled wall and ran his fingers over the carvings. There was absolute silence in the room while he searched for the right place, absolute silence in the whole palace, when suddenly Kei-lin heard a sound which filled her with intense horror. It was coming from outside the palace.

Earth-mute heard it too at the same moment and his eyes filled with fear. He did not know what it was, but Kei-lin knew and she turned pale with dismay.

She whispered to Earth-mute, "It's the dragon snoring!" Earth-mute signed to Heaven-deaf.

"He'll wake up Wen Chang," gasped Heaven-deaf. Quickly, run out and stop him." But it was too late.

As Kei-lin hurried to the door of the room Wen Chang came stomping down the hall. He carried a huge swinging oil lamp which lit up Kei-lin's terrified face and showed him at once what was happening. Lan Tan Tin vanished, but Heaven-deaf and Earth-mute could not do that. The enormous god caught the two little men, one in each hand, and shook them.

"What are you up to in my most secret room in the middle of the night?" he roared. "I shall throw you into the deepest dungeons in the palace for this disobedience, and as for you," this to Kei-lin, "I'll boil you in my soup."

But Kei-lin did not wait to hear any more from

the furious god. She dodged past him, flew down the stairs and out into the courtyard. She screamed at the snoring dragon and beat him with her fists. "Wake up," she cried, "wake up and let's go quickly. Quickly, or we'll all be lost."

The astonished dragon did not stop to argue, for he could hear the panic in Kei-lin's voice. He rose into the air at once, with Kei-lin hanging on to him for dear life, and headed away from the palace. Looking back, Kei-lin could see the figure of the God of Literature with the lantern in one hand and the two hapless servants in the other. He seemed to be shouting something up at her but Kei-lin did not stop to listen. She urged the dragon on and they streaked through the skies.

"What happened?" shouted the dragon.

"You snored and woke up Wen Chang," Kei-lin wailed. "Oh, why did you have to be so stupid!"

"I didn't know I was snoring," the dragon replied.

"You should know by now," Kei-lin shouted. "You always snore. You've snored for thousands of years. You shouldn't have fallen asleep."

"I know," said the dragon, and he didn't say anything more. Kei-lin knew he was feeling badly which made her feel worse, and she wished she hadn't said anything about his snoring.

She was recovering from her great fright and was beginning to feel ashamed of having run away and left Heaven-deaf and Earth-mute, those kind little men, all alone with the angry god. As her fright faded she felt worse and worse, and finally she called to the dragon:

"Don't go so fast, I think we should turn back—or—well—I don't know what—but I feel so badly about the little servants."

The dragon lessened speed. "I can't stop now," he called back. "We've left the Great Bear and we have to reach some other place before I can stop."

"Oh, but then we should go back," cried Kei-lin. "I can't leave those poor creatures without any help. That Wen Chang was furious."

"What can we do even if we do go back?" asked the dragon.

"Well, surely you can go and rescue them," Kei-lin said. "You're so big. You could overpower the god."

"You should know better than that," said the dragon. "I am only a dragon. Strong and large, but still only a dragon. And Wen Chang is a god. I can't overpower him. If I am to get my own way with Wen Chang or any other god, I have to do it peacefully—perhaps by persuading them. I can't just go and knock them about because I'm bigger. You should know that. Not gods."

"Yes, I suppose I do know that," Kei-lin said, sighing, "but we should be able to do something. Oh, everything's gone wrong. Why is that Wen Chang so unkind? Oh, what shall I do about Linza?" And she felt so unhappy that she began to sob and reached for the large red handkerchief which the dragon always kept hidden behind one of his scales for just such an emergency.

THE CONTEST

THEY FLEW for a long time in silence except for Kei-lin's sniffles, and even those abated after some time, and at last the dragon found a convenient place on which to land. It was beginning to get light and Kei-lin looked around for something to eat but there wasn't anything, so they sat and looked at each other gloomily while the skies got brighter and brighter.

"Now let's think about this carefully," said the dragon. "There must be some solution. Wen Chang won't tell you anything because he doesn't care about anyone being unhappy. This is because he's unhappy himself. So the solution to our problem is obvious. We have to find some way of making Wen Chang happy."

Kei-lin didn't say anything.

"Now," continued the dragon, "what are the things that make people happy?"

"Well," Kei-lin said slowly, "at Linza's wedding everyone was wishing her health, long life, and prosperity."

47

"Health, long life, and prosperity," the dragon repeated. "Wen Chang has health, that's obvious enough. And of course being a god he has not only long life, but eternity. Neither of these seems to make him happy. And learning certainly isn't making him happy. So the only thing left—and which he certainly hasn't got judging by the state the palace is in—is wealth. He is certainly not a rich god." He stopped for a while and sucked one of his claws thoughtfully.

"So," Kei-lin prompted him.

"So we have to try riches," the dragon said.

"Riches!" Kei-lin repeated. "Who has riches? I know my uncle is well enough off. He is the headman in our village. But he certainly doesn't have what you'd call riches."

"No," said the dragon, "nobody that you would know would have the kind of riches we would need. We would have to go to the source of all riches. We would have to visit the God of Riches."

"The God of Riches!" Kei-lin repeated.

"The God of Riches," the dragon said. "I have never seen him myself, nor visited his domain, but I understand that he has so much wealth that he doesn't know what to do with it. Do you know, the branches of the trees in his garden are strings of coins and the fruit are ingots of gold. All you have to do is to shake them down. And then he has a magic casket full of gold and silver, and no matter how much money you take out of it, it always fills up again."

Kei-lin's eyes were popping out of her head. "Why," she cried, "of course we should visit him. I'm sure when we tell him our whole story he will give us some of his riches. He must be a very happy god and willing to help us. Do you know where his domain is?"

"I think I'll be able to find it," the dragon replied.

They flew for a long time and then in the distance saw a garden enclosed by what seemed like an endless wall. The dragon and Kei-lin alighted some distance away under a spreading tree.

"I could fly right over the wall," the dragon said, "but it would not be right. We'll knock on the gate and go in, in the usual way. Let's walk around the wall and see if we can find a gate."

The wall wound on and on, sometimes for long, straight stretches, and sometimes turning quite sharp corners. It was at one of these sharp corners that they heard a fearful roar, and as they stood there, quite frozen with fright, a monstrous beast loomed up before them. With one bound Kei-lin leaped up onto the dragon's back and he took off without a backward glance. The roaring of the fearful beast faded away, and when they could hear it no more the dragon alighted.

Kei-lin rolled off the dragon's back and lay on the grass, still trembling.

The dragon said, after a long period of silence, "That wasn't very dignified of me—taking off like that."

"What else could we do?" Kei-lin said. "It was so unexpected."

"He must be the guardian of the gate," the dragon said after a while. "Come to think of it now, I had heard that there was such a guardian at the Gate of Riches, but I did not know he was so ferocious. He must have been just by the gate."

"He was frightful," Kei-lin said, shuddering. "A fearful monster."

"He was," the dragon agreed. "You'd think that he'd at least give one a chance to say something." They lay in silence for quite a while. Then Kei-lin said:

"But you know, he wasn't any more fearful than you."

"What!" cried the dragon in an amazed voice.

"Oh, please don't be offended," Kei-lin cried. "I know you're really very good-looking for a dragon— and I just love you because you're so kind and good—but still, you are a dragon, and when other people look at you they must think you are quite fearful."

The dragon sighed. "I suppose they do," he agreed.

"Besides that," Kei-lin went on, "the monster wasn't any bigger than you. In fact if you count your tail I think he was shorter. I'm sure he wasn't any stronger than you. He just made a lot of noise."

The dragon sat up. "Kei-lin," he said sternly, "what exactly are you getting at?"

Kei-lin flushed. "Well, what I was really think-ing," she said, "was that you could frighten that monster just as much as—as—" she didn't want to say "as much as he frightened you," so she said "as much as he startled us."

"Well . . ." said the dragon, settling down into the grass again. "Well . . ."

"What can you do?" asked Kei-lin after a pause. "Can you blow fire?"

"No," said the dragon. "I can't. Not really. Only a little smoke now and then."

"Well practice," said Kei-lin, getting up. "Prac-tice. Maybe you can. You haven't tried for so long. Maybe you can blow fire. And that would terrorize the monster. Come on, try."

"Very well," said the dragon, "I'll try." He got up a little unwillingly and took a deep breath. He blew. Nothing happened except that some of the trees bent down as if before a heavy gale. "Try again," Kei-lin said, "come on, try hard." The dragon obeyed. He blew a little harder and a little harder. The more he blew the stronger he seemed to become. No fire came out of his mouth, but his breath became very hot and grew stronger and stronger. Kei-lin stood behind him, fearing that he would blow her across the countryside if she came in the line of his breath. At last the dragon blew so hard that the trees in front of him snapped right off their roots and fell to the ground.

"You're wonderful," cried Kei-lin, "just wonder-

ful! You don't need to blow fire. You can just blow
at that monster and he'll be mowed down. Come
on, we have nothing to fear."

"All right," said the dragon, "but let me have a
bit of a rest." He lay down, gasping a little. He was
secretly feeling very proud of being able to blow so
hard.

When he was fully rested, Kei-lin tugged at the
scales on his wing. "Come on, let's not waste any
time. Let's go," she urged.

"I don't think you should go," said the dragon.
"I think you should stay here safely while I go. You
never know. Things might not go too well."

"Oh stop talking like that," Kei-lin cried. "You
must have confidence in yourself. Nothing will
happen to me. Of course I'm coming with you."

"No," said the dragon, and he was quite determined, so determined that Kei-lin saw it was useless
arguing with him. "You stay here."

"Well, not quite here," she said, "I won't go
right up to the monster with you, but take me
closer so that I can see what happens. I want to see
you blowing the monster away."

"Very well," said the dragon, "but not too
close." They flew off in the direction of the Domain
of Riches. When they were fairly close to the gate
the dragon deposited Kei-lin behind a little hill.
"You stay here until I tell you the coast is clear," he
told her.

But Kei-lin did not obey the dragon. As soon as
his back was turned, she crept closer to the gate,
just to see what would happen.

The dragon approached the gate and shouted in a large voice. "I seek entrance into the Domain of Riches." For an answer he heard the same fearful roar they had heard earlier in the day, and the monster guardian of the gate appeared before him.

"No one enters the Domain of Riches," roared the monster.

"I do not come as a thief," the dragon replied. "I come to visit the God of Riches."

"No one comes to visit the God," replied the monster. "He needs no visitors."

"You are not very hospitable, I must say," the dragon replied. "You are a disgrace to our Chinese traditions."

The monster growled, gnashed his teeth with rage, and threw himself on the dragon. But the dragon was prepared. He blew. The monster's rush was immediately halted. The dragon drew a deep breath, advanced, and prepared to blow again. But then an unexpected thing happened. The monster blew back at the dragon. His breath was so strong that Kei-lin was picked up off the ground and whirled away. Fortunately she landed in a bush, and apart from scratches was unharmed, but she saw right away that she had to find shelter. This she did in a shallow ditch, and she peeped out over the side of the ditch once in a while when the dragon was doing the blowing, to see how things were going.

Every time the dragon blew, the monster was pinned against the gate behind him, gasping for breath, but when the dragon stopped to draw breath, the monster blew the dragon several hundred feet away from the wall. So they continued blowing at each other, while all around them the landscape was gradually leveled. Bushes and boulders flew about, trees bent to the ground and finally snapped, and the earth blew around in great clouds of dust and small gravel. Kei-lin had never seen such a terrible storm. Soon she couldn't even see anything any more, for the air grew so thick with dust, and she just hoped that nothing would blow into her ditch and crush her. She saw how wrong she had been to disobey the dragon. She should have stayed behind the little hill where he had left her.

On and on raged the storm, and Kei-lin thought they would never stop blowing at each other, when all at once there was a loud gasping groan and then silence. Kei-lin started to crawl out of the ditch. If it was the dragon who had collapsed, then she was done for. It would be her own fault—she should never have urged him to go. But who would ever have thought the monster would blow back like that?

Then through the still whirling dust Kei-lin saw the familiar figure of the dragon and heard his voice, how dear to her ears, calling, rather hoarsely, "Kei-lin, where are you?"

"Here I am," cried Kei-lin, running toward him and throwing her arms around one of his great legs. "Oh, how glad I am to see you!"

"Kei-lin," said the dragon crossly, "why didn't you stay behind the little hill where I left you?"

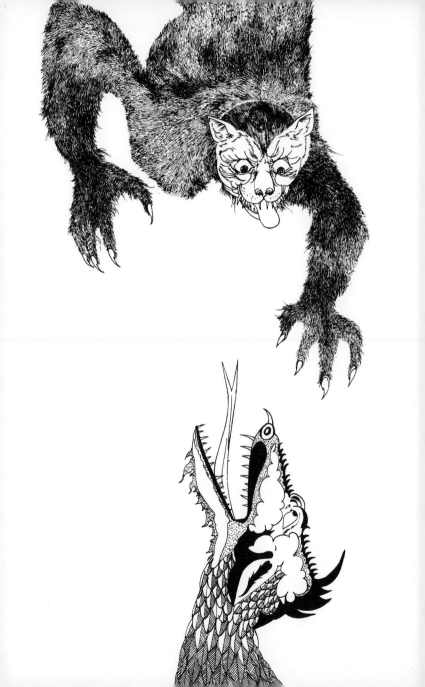

"I wanted to see what would happen—how did I know that the monster would blow back? I never thought of that."

"Ah, but I did," said the dragon. "Anyway, come on, let's hurry. He's in a dead faint. I don't know how long he'll be like that, but we must get in through the gate before he comes to. Come on."

THE DOMAIN OF RICHES

ONCE THE MONSTER was out of the way it was not difficult to get through the huge gate into the Domain of Riches. They did not even have to open the main gate itself as there was a smaller one set in the side which simply swung on its hinges without a lock of any kind. This they entered and looked down the long avenue of very strange trees, which Kei-lin recognized as some of those the dragon had described to her. The branches of these trees were indeed strings of coins and the fruit that hung on them were round lumps of gold. They proceeded down the avenue, staring at the shimmering trees, when Kei-lin noticed another odd thing. The stones and the pebbles underfoot were glinting and shining like no pebbles she had ever seen. She picked one up and realized that it was a ruby. She picked up another, and it was an emerald.

"Look," she cried to the dragon, "the pebbles are all jewels. Oh, aren't they lovely." She fell to her knees, sweeping together the lovely colored stones, picking them up in her cupped hands and then dribbling them through her fingers. "Oh, how I'd like to take some home!"

"Kei-lin," said the dragon, "we've come here as guests. We can't walk out with our pockets full of our host's possessions."

"My pockets you mean," Kei-lin corrected him. "You haven't got any. But you're right," she sighed, and getting up she followed the dragon up the path.

On and on they walked. The avenue twisted and turned, and took them here and there and everywhere, but nowhere could they see anything like a palace or a house of any sort where the God of Riches could be living. At last they made one last turn, and to their dismay found themselves on the same long avenue they had first entered, and sure enough, at the very end was the entrance gate.

"Oh dear," cried Kei-lin, "we've simply come in a circle."

"Let's try again," said the dragon, "we must have missed some turning. It can't be as senseless as all that. Let's go back."

They went back, Kei-lin feeling a little tired and depressed by now. She picked up some of the jewels and played with them in her hand, watching the sun sparkle on them, when suddenly there was a great whoosh and she found herself flying to one side of the path, the dragon landing nearly on top of her, while she caught a glimpse of a white shape flying by them.

"Whatever happened?" she gasped when she had caught her breath.

Now the air was filled with cries, like the neighs of a horse in distress, and following the dragon's gaze Kei-lin gasped. A beautiful, perfectly white unicorn, the white shape she had seen flying past them, had run his horn into the trunk of one of the trees lining the avenue, and was held thus, imprisoned.

"He nearly ran one of us through," the dragon said. "It was a good thing I wasn't playing with colored pebbles and was on the lookout." He spoke rather gruffly, for he had been very startled.

"You mean you saw him coming and pulled me out of the way, just in time?" Kei-lin asked.

"Only just in time," the dragon replied. "He came so fast—around that corner. The God of Riches certainly keeps his domain well guarded."

"I'm glad you weren't playing with pebbles," said Kei-lin gratefully.

They walked toward the unicorn, who tried to get a glimpse of them out of a corner of his eye but could not, for they were behind him. He sobbed in distress, and his whole beautiful body shook with fear.

Kei-lin felt sorry for him, even though only a moment before it seemed that he had nearly run her through with his horn.

"You're certainly not very hospitable around here," the dragon said, still grumpily. "Can't you say a friendly word to anyone? Fancy trying to run a little girl through with your horn."

The unicorn trembled more than ever. "And indeed," Kei-lin thought, "the dragon is a fierce-looking creature."

"Why did you do that?" asked the dragon. The unicorn tried to speak. A gurgly sound came from his throat. At last he said:

"I wasn't trying to run her through. I was only trying to frighten you."

"Well," said the dragon, "you certainly came close enough."

"It's my duty," continued the unicorn. "I would never have done it. I mean I would never have run you through. But I have to pretend that I might. No one is allowed into the Domain of Riches."

"But we didn't come to steal anything," the dragon pointed out. "We only came as guests. That should have been clear enough to you."

"No one is allowed into the Domain of Riches," repeated the unicorn, as though it was a lesson he had learned very well. "Not even as guests. Don't you understand? This is an evil place. We are trying to protect you from *it*. Not it from you."

"Why is it an evil place?" asked Kei-lin. "I think it's the most beautiful place I've ever seen."

"No one can leave the Domain of Riches feeling happy," said the unicorn. "Even if you were given some of the riches, you would only want more, and more, and more. There would never be any end to your wanting. And so you would be miserable to the end of your lives. And even if you had the whole of the Domain of Riches to yourself, it would not make you happy. Look at the God of Riches. He is a miserable creature."

"A miserable creature!" Kei-lin repeated, and she looked at the dragon, deep dismay filling her eyes.

"Please free me from the tree," the unicorn begged them. "I know I frightened you, but that's what I'm supposed to do. I won't frighten you again, I promise."

"Do free him," Kei-lin begged the dragon.

"Not until you promise to take us to see the God of the Riches," replied the dragon.

"I will take you to see him," replied the unicorn, "but you won't find him a very pleasant fellow. He lives in a dark cave and never cuts his hair."

"In a cave!" Kei-lin repeated. "No wonder we couldn't find him. We were looking for a palace."

"No," said the unicorn sadly. "The god is tired of all his riches. He can have anything he wants in the world—anything that can be bought with money—and so he doesn't want any of it."

"He must be a very odd person," Kei-lin said. And then she added to the dragon, "Come on, free the unicorn."

"Very well," said the dragon. He took hold of the unicorn's horn with one of his great claws, leaned against the tree, and had soon pulled the horn free of the trunk.

"Well, come along now," the dragon said. "Let's go to the God of Riches."

"Very well," cried the unicorn, and he bounded away through the trees with the dragon and Kei-lin hurrying after him.

After they had been following the unicorn for quite a long time he suddenly turned right off the avenue onto a little path among the magic trees, a little path Kei-lin had not noticed on her first trip around the Domain of Riches. It could scarcely be called a path; it was just a place where the trees seemed to be a little thinner. He led them along this until the trees ceased and the ground became rather hilly. They rounded one of the rises and came upon the mouth of a dark cave.

The unicorn paused at the mouth of the cave and called, "Tsai Shen, Tsai Shen."

There was silence for a long time, and at last a faint and faraway voice replied:

"Who is it that calls me?"

"It is I, the sacred unicorn."

"What do you want with me?" asked the weary-sounding voice.

"I have brought two guests to visit you," replied the unicorn. "They are very anxious to see you."

"Guests!" came the echo from the cave. Then there was silence.

"Maybe you'd like to go in and see him yourself," the unicorn suggested. "You'd have to go alone because the dragon is too big to move around in the narrow passage at the end of the cave."

"Well . . ." Kei-lin did not like this idea at all. The cave looked very dark indeed and the god did not seem too welcoming. How would she ever get out again, especially if the dragon couldn't get in to save her? "I don't think—" she began.

"There's nothing else for it," said the unicorn. "You see, he simply won't come out to see anyone. You must not be frightened, because he is not a fierce god. He is simply very weary of everything. He is a very, very tired god. If he doesn't want to talk to you he simply won't and you'll come out again."

"Well . . . ?" said Kei-lin again looking at the dragon. He looked back at her but did not urge her on. Kei-lin knew she had to make her own decision. It was a matter of either going into the cave and trying to speak to the god, or of simply going home and leaving poor Linza to her fate.

"All right," said Kei-lin at last. "I'll try." She reached up her jacket sleeve and pressed Linza's bracelet. It gave her some courage.

"At the end of this first cave," said the unicorn, "you will find a passageway, and at the end of the passageway is the cave of the God of Riches. Good luck."

Kei-lin stepped into the dark cave. Through the gloom, at the other end, she saw what looked like the beginnings of a passageway. She walked toward it. The ground under her feet was soft and spongy. The daylight was now completely cut off, but after a while her eyes became used to the gloom and she could see that the passageway was very narrow. She walked along it, wary of pitfalls, and at last found her way into another large cave.

This cave was partially lighted from somewhere up above. There were the remains of a fire in the center, something that looked like a bed of leaves and bracken in one corner, and right at the back of the cave, seated on a stone, his beard flowing to the floor, sat a pitiable, hunched-up figure.

By the light that filtered into the cave Kei-lin saw that the god was very old and wizened. His clothes were very shabby, and his eyes were closed, as though in sleep.

She came nearer and gave a little cough. The old god continued to doze. "Excuse me, sir," Kei-lin said very politely and bowed, although he wasn't looking at her at all.

"Please sir," said Kei-lin a little more loudly, "please speak to me."

At last the old man stirred. He opened his eyes and lifted up his head. He observed Kei-lin very wearily.

"Whatever are you doing here?" he asked. "And how did you ever get in?"

"I came with my dragon," said Kei-lin.

"What a story," said the old god. "I don't believe a word of it. Why, I don't even believe you're real. You're just another of those dreams the God of Sleep sends me every so often. My best friend, you know, the God of Sleep."

"No, no, indeed I'm not," cried Kei-lin. "And if you'll only listen to my story, I'm sure you'll be willing to help me."

"I don't believe you're real," said the old god. "Come here, close to me, so that I can touch you." And Kei-lin, shaking in every limb, approached close to the god, so that he could touch her.

A VERY WEARY GOD

THE GOD put out long, thin, wizened fingers and touched the hem of Kei-lin's jacket. "Yes," he said, nodding his head thoughtfully, "I suppose you are real after all. But you know, I do have a great many dreams. I dream eternity away." He looked at Kei-lin so sadly that she almost felt like crying. His face must have a thousand lines on it at least, she thought. And because she was so disappointed to find the God of Riches so sad, a tear did actually escape and roll down her cheek.

The old god continued to look at her thoughtfully, as another and yet another tear slipped and rolled down her cheek, and Kei-lin wiped her eyes with the sleeve of her jacket. "Come and sit down here," he said at last, very kindly. "Come and sit here beside me and tell me what you are crying about." He patted a smooth stone close to him, and Kei-lin sat down and began to tell him her story.

"And so," she ended, "we thought that if we could possibly get some riches for the God of

66

Literature, he would be happy and tell us how we could overcome the wicked god's spell. But now I see that you've got all the riches in the world, and you're so terribly weary of everything, and so sad."

The god sat very still for a very long time, until Kei-lin thought he had fallen asleep again. His head was bent and his beard touched the floor. But at last he lifted his head and looked at her out of his tired eyes.

"I have been doing the same as the God of Literature," he told her. "I too spent thousands of years looking for happiness. I was sure that riches would bring me happiness, and so I gathered riches, and I was so successful that they have even taken over from me and are multiplying all by themselves. I can't even get rid of my riches. The more I spend the more they grow. I can buy anything I want in the whole wide world. And I don't want any of it. Don't ask me why—I don't know. I have been searching for happiness through riches and I simply can't find it."

"But there must be some way," Kei-lin cried. "There must be some way to find happiness, some sure way. Oh, it's terribly important to us. Can't you see how important? The dragon fought, and I came into this dark cave although I was terribly afraid, and we did it because it's so important. Oh, if you knew Linza you would understand. You would find some way to help us."

"Dear little Kei-lin," said the old god, "I do understand how important this must be to you.

Yes, I do indeed. But I do not think that riches are going to solve your problem. Of course you can have my riches. You can have as much as you want. But no amount of riches is going to help Wen Chang. I can assure you of that. I am very old and I know."

"But what shall we do then?" cried Kei-lin.

The old man once again plunged into thought, his head dropping nearly to his knees. "There is only one thing I can think of," he said, "but I don't know whether it will be of any use to you." He looked up at Kei-lin, and she saw that his eyes were clouding over as though he was about to drift away into sleep again. "What is it?" she asked sharply, in an effort to keep him awake.

"Go to the very source of happiness itself. Go to Fu Shen, the God of Happiness, and ask him for his secret. Perhaps you will be luckier than any of us have been."

"But have you ever asked him?" cried Kei-lin.

"No. We have tried of course. But none of us has been successful. You see, the queer fact of the matter is that no one, no one at all, has ever seen the God of Happiness for longer than a second at a time—certainly not long enough to ask him what his secret was."

"But why do you think I would be more successful?" Kei-lin cried. "If all the important gods like you have failed, why should I be more successful? I'm only a little girl."

The god spoke slowly. It seemed an effort for

him to say each word: "That's—the very—reason—why—you—might succeed—because you're a little girl," he said. And then he fell asleep.

Kei-lin could see that he was really asleep this time. She looked at him with a feeling of great pity. She wanted to thank him, she wanted to say good-bye, but he could not hear her any more.

"Thank you," she tried, "good-bye," but there was no answer. At last she lifted his beard gently from out of the dust at his feet and laid it across his knee and then left the cave.

The passageway did not seem nearly as frightening as it had at first, and in no time at all she had rejoined the dragon and the unicorn. She told them what had happened. "What is the sense of going to see a god whom no one ever sees?" she asked. "Oh, how hopeless it all seems."

But then Kei-lin began to think of Linza and of all the kind people bewitched in the town of Senfu, and she knew that she couldn't possibly let any chance go by without at any rate trying. The dragon sat hunched on the ground watching her, and when she lifted up her head and looked at him, he knew that she had decided to go.

"Good for you," he said, even before she said anything.

"Have you ever been there before?" asked Kei-lin.

"No, I have not," replied the dragon. "Oddly enough, I've never thought of looking for happiness—always too busy, somehow. But it won't be any trouble finding the place, I'm sure. I've heard of it often enough, and of people who have gone there to try to find the secret of happiness."

"And did anyone ever find it?" asked Kei-lin.

"Who knows?" replied the dragon. "Perhaps they did. I never asked them, for I wasn't looking for it myself."

"Why don't you stay and eat with me, and have a rest," the unicorn suggested. "The journey to the realm of happiness is a long one and you will need all your strength."

"That is a good idea," the dragon agreed. "I must say, all that blowing certainly exhausted me." When they had eaten the dragon fell fast asleep and Kei-lin dozed too. But she could not sleep for long because she was too anxious to continue their journey.

At last the dragon awoke, refreshed and ready for their next long flight. The beautiful white unicorn looked at them sadly. "I hope you understand why I tried to keep you out of here," he said. "I do not want anyone else to become like my master, the God of Riches."

"We do understand," Kei-lin said, and her eyes filled with tears to think of having to say good-bye to him.

"Do not be sad for me," said the unicorn, as though he could read her thoughts. "We all have to live out our own destinies. And one day I shall be free from this place."

"When will that be?" asked Kei-lin eagerly, for

she thought how lovely it would be to have the unicorn as a pet to play with in the fields at home.

"When it is no longer dangerous to give men all the riches in the world."

Kei-lin did not quite understand what he meant, but she saw that there was some hope for him, so she felt a little happier.

"Good-bye then," she said, preparing to climb on the dragon's back.

"I have a gift for you," said the unicorn. "I want you to have this as a memento of your visit to us." And he placed a small box in her hand.

Kei-lin looked with delight at the unexpected present. She liked presents more than anything else in the world, and this was indeed a lovely one. The box was made of ivory with thin tracings of gold all over, and had a golden hasp.

"Open it," said the unicorn. Kei-lin opened it. Within, resting on shining white satin, lay three emeralds. The sun caught them and they glittered.

"Oh, how beautiful," Kei-lin gasped. "Why, thank you very much." She closed the little box securely and placed it in her pocket, buttoning the flap over it. "I shall always treasure it," she said, and her eyes filled with tears again. The dragon hastily handed her the red handkerchief, which made her laugh a little, and in another moment they had risen high over the Domain of Riches, and were sailing away into the blue sky. Behind them the white unicorn stood among the gleaming trees of the Domain of Riches, looking after them.

The sun set while they were traveling and they flew on through the dark silent night.

At last, in the distance, an island of mountains appeared, and as they approached Kei-lin saw what seemed to be a bank of clouds on one of the mountain ledges. The dragon landed quite close to the bank and Kei-lin looked at him in surprise. "This is the home of the God of Happiness," said the dragon.

She thought then that it was a palace wrapped in mists, but she soon saw that this was not the case. To her dismay she saw that there was nothing but mists, forming and reforming constantly. Where there had been a fine curved roof a moment ago was now a square tower, and a long gallery of windows had changed to a graceful bridge.

"Why," she cried, "how shall we ever get in there? Look, it's changing all the time."

"Of course," said the dragon, "but don't worry about that. It won't be as difficult as it looks." Together they walked toward what appeared to be an outer wall and in the direction of what seemed at that moment to be a gate.

"You'll have to go in without me," said the dragon. "There is nothing frightening in the home of the God of Happiness, though you might find things—well, a little curious."

"Very well," said Kei-lin rather uncertainly, and even as she spoke the gate in front of them disappeared and in its place was a lovely, moon-shaped bridge.

"Go on," the dragon urged her. "Can't you see, that's their way of saying come in—the gate has disappeared."

"Very well," said Kei-lin, putting one foot on the bridge. She felt that she could not be at all sure that the bridge might not suddenly disappear and leave her in a lake of lotus lilies. But the bridge held and was remarkably strong under her feet for something that seemed made of mists, and in a few moments she found herself on the other side in a glade of green grass and trees.

"Now," she said to herself, "I must start looking for the God of Happiness. I wonder where he can be. He must be here somewhere."

She walked among the trees and across smooth lawns for quite a long time, expecting at any moment to see her host, but there was no sign of him anywhere. At last she turned a corner and came upon a garden.

It was the most beautiful garden she had ever seen. "Why," she cried in delight, "I've never seen such a lovely garden. Never in my whole life."

There were flowers of every color and every shape and size, and the air was filled with their perfume. Kei-lin ran from a glowing red rose to a proud white lily, from a blazing azalea bush to a carpet of darling forget-me-nots, touching and smelling and marveling. This was a garden which the seasons had forgotten, for every flower in the world bloomed there.

Kei-lin shook a branch of orange blossoms gently,

and the scented white petals floated down on her face. Laughing, she fell on her knees and buried her nose in a cluster of hyacinths. And then, just as she was about to get up, she suddenly knew that she was not alone.

THE SECRET

SHE HAD HEARD nothing and she had seen nothing, but she knew. She turned her head quickly, and there behind her stood a tall, shadowy figure. For some reason she did not feel the slightest bit afraid of him. She jumped to her feet and cried:

"Oh, I'm so happy. I've never seen such flowers —I never thought there was anything like this—but if you please, sir, I'm looking for the God of Happiness. Do you think you could—" But she never finished her sentence, for even as she spoke the shadowy figure vanished, and as she looked around her, so had all the flowers.

She found herself in a narrow passageway with windows on either side. She looked out of one of the windows, hoping to see the lovely garden outside, but there was nothing there but a stone courtyard. For a moment she felt like crying, for the flowers had been so glorious, but then she remembered that she was there with a purpose and not to spend her time admiring beautiful flowers, and so she started down the passageway.

At the other end there was a door. She knocked, and when there was no answer she pushed it aside and stepped into the room. Then she gasped.

She was in a dolls' house. Kei-lin had never seen a dolls' house, not even a small one, and this one was so big that she had stepped right into it. The dolls she and Mei-dee played with were simple things, but these, surely, were the dolls of the emperor's daughter herself.

They were dressed in the most elaborate costumes and were seated on rosewood furniture which was as finely carved as any furniture in a palace. For a few moments she stared, wide-eyed, then she dropped to her knees and started to play with the dolls.

"You little dears," she cried to a couple of babies whose hair was tied up on the top of their heads with red bows, "you darling, darling little things." There were tiny bowls and chopsticks on the tables, and real blankets on the beds, and the cupboards had spare clothing in them. Kei-lin decided to change the babies' clothes. "I could play here forever," she thought to herself. "I'll put out their meals and wash their dishes and put them to bed." The pleasure she felt reached right down to her toenails.

It was at the moment when she was feeling her happiest—she had just dressed the second baby and set him down ready for his lunch—that she knew again she was not alone. She looked up to see the stranger laughing down at her. And this time she suddenly realized who he was.

"Oh, dear God of Happiness," she cried, jumping to her feet, "please, please don't disappear again. I am looking for the secret of happiness. It's terribly important . . ." But she never finished her sentence. The stranger vanished, and with him the lovely playroom, and Kei-lin found herself outside the misty walls, beside the waiting dragon.

"How did you get here?" he asked. "I didn't see you coming through the gate."

"What gate?" asked Kei-lin. "There's no gate. It turned into a bridge."

"Well, it's a gate again," said the dragon, and so it was. Kei-lin sighed with disappointment.

"You don't look too happy," the dragon said. "I suppose you did not find the secret of happiness."

Kei-lin shrugged.

"What happened?" asked the dragon.

"I—don't know—exactly," Kei-lin said.

"Why don't you go back in?" asked the dragon. "Have another try."

"It won't be any use," Kei-lin said. "It'll just happen the same way . . ."

"What will happen the same way?"

"Please don't talk right now," Kei-lin said. "I just feel as if I've been told something, but I haven't quite understood it, and I think if I'm quiet for a little while I'll suddenly understand it."

"What shall we do then?" asked the dragon.

"Nothing," said Kei-lin. "Just be quiet."

The dragon felt a bit huffy so he lay down and rested his snout on his paws. After a few moments he fell asleep. He snored gently. Kei-lin sat quietly. She was not exactly thinking. She was just reliving the events of the past hour because she knew that somehow an important message had been given her and it was up to her to grasp it. She sat for a long time. Then she gave a loud cry and thumped the dragon on his snout.

He snorted with rage and leaped up.

"Listen, just listen to me," she cried before he had time to say anything. "I've got it! Yes, yes, I've really got it. Now listen.

"First I looked and looked for the God of Happiness but I couldn't find him anywhere. Then I went into that glorious flower garden, and I was perfectly happy. I could have stayed there forever. The God of Happiness appeared, and the moment I remembered that I had to look for happiness, for the secret of happiness, he disappeared and all my happiness with him. And the same thing happened in the dolls' house. Don't you see? Don't you see?" she continued, hammering the dragon with her little fists.

"I don't see anything," said the dragon grumpily, "and I'm telling you this, that if you ever thump me—"

"But you great big, silly thing," cried Kei-lin, jumping up and down in excitement and hugging the dragon's legs by turn, "don't you see that *is* the secret of happiness."

"I must confess," said the dragon, "maybe it's because I was very sleepy and was wakened so rudely, but I don't have the faintest notion of what you are talking about."

"The secret of happiness, the secret of happiness, that's what I'm talking about," Kei-lin cried. "Come on, we must go back to the God of Literature. We'll tell him the secret of happiness and he'll help us rescue Linza. Come on, hurry up."

"Kei-lin," said the dragon, "I'm not budging from here until you explain exactly what you mean."

"The secret of happiness," said Kei-lin, and her eyes grew very round and bright, "is simply *never to look for it*. If you forget all about looking for it then it's just suddenly there, but the moment you remember that you have to look for happiness, it disappears. It's as simple as that."

The dragon stared at her, rubbing his snout thoughtfully.

"Come along, come along, let's go," she cried, "I know exactly what I'm talking about." She climbed on the dragon's back and he rose into the air, still without saying anything. It was only after they had been flying for quite some time that the dragon called back to her:

"I don't know why I never thought of that before," he said.

As they approached the Great Bear and the palace of the God of Literature, Kei-lin began to feel nervous.

"He will probably still be very angry with me," she thought. "I will be alone. I won't have Heaven-deaf and Earth-mute to help me."

The palace of Wen Chang looked as dismal as it had when they had first seen it. They landed in the courtyard, and Kei-lin looked up the tall, forbidding stone steps which led to the door. "If he throws me out, it'll be awful tumbling down all those steps," she thought. Aloud she said to the dragon, "You'd

better not go too far away. You know he's probably
still quite angry." And in spite of the knowledge
that the dragon would be in the courtyard, Kei-lin's
heart beat very fast as she mounted the steps and
knocked on the door.

There was no answer, so Kei-lin tried it, and
finding it unlocked she pushed it open and peered
in. There was the dim hallway, with the staircase at
one side and the doors all around it, and at the far
end the panel that she knew led into the god's own
room. She stepped fearfully into the hallway. There
was no sound anywhere. Kei-lin walked softly down
the hall.

At the door of the god's room she stood uncertainly for a long time, gathering up her courage.
Then at last she knocked.

"Who's there?" came the big voice of the god.

Kei-lin pushed aside the panel and stepped into
the dim room.

"So, it's you," said the god. Yes, Kei-lin could see
that he was still angry.

"Do you realize," said the god, "that I could just
take you up in this enormous hand and squeeze the
life out of you?"

Kei-lin nodded.

"Then what are you doing here again?"

"I've brought something for you," said Kei-lin in
a tiny voice.

"What have you brought for me? What can a
poor little mortal like you possibly bring a great god
like me?"

"It's just an idea," said Kei-lin.

"An idea!" repeated the god. "Do you know that I've got a million, million ideas stacked away in this palace? What idea can you possibly bring me?"

"I've brought you the secret of happiness," Kei-lin said. There was silence in the great room for a moment. Then the huge god thumped his fist down on his table so that pens and scrolls flew in every direction.

"What impertinence!" he shouted. "You will be thrown into the prison together with those two foolish slave of mine," and he swung around in his chair and made as though to grab Kei-lin.

CHUCHUCHAN

KEI-LIN dodged behind a chair to avoid his hands. "But listen to me for a moment," she begged desperately, and she looked so much in earnest that even the angry god paused in his raging and looked at her more closely.

"You've been looking for happiness for thousands of years, in all the wisest books in the world, and you haven't found it. And that's because it's no use looking for happiness. The only way to find happiness is *not* to look for it."

Kei-lin's words rang on the air and they repeated themselves over and over in her own head, "The only way to find happiness is not to look for it, the only way . . . ," over and over again.

After the god had said nothing for a very long time Kei-lin said in a whisper, "I know it sounds silly. But it's true. It happened to me."

The god peered more and more closely at Kei-lin.

"What did you say?" he said, and his voice was

scarcely above a whisper. "Say it again—the only way to find happiness is . . . ?"

"Not to look for it," Kei-lin repeated.

And then to her relief the god thumped his heavy fist on the table again and burst into a resounding guffaw of laughter. "And to think of all the years I've wasted looking for it," he roared. "Little mortal, why didn't you come here sooner?"

"You mean you really believe me?" Kei-lin croaked.

"Believe you?" the god repeated. "There's nothing to believe. It is suddenly perfectly clear to me. Why even just the thought of never having to look for happiness again makes me feel happy. For the first time in my life I'm happy, because I don't have to look for happiness. I can read my writings just for fun!" And he roared with laughter again. Then he sobered a little.

"There's just one thing that bothers me," he said, "I just don't know how I never thought of it myself."

"You probably would have, in time," Kei-lin said kindly.

"Yes, yes, that's true," the god agreed quickly. "I would have, in time. Doubtless, I was too busy searching. But now, little mortal, what can I do for you in return? I want to do all sorts of kind things now because I'm beginning to feel happier and happier. To think of never having to look for happiness again!" And he sighed a great sigh of relief.

"I think you know what you can do in return,"

said Kei-lin. "First you must release Heaven-deaf and Earth-mute. And then you must help me to break Chuchuchan's spell."

"Of course, of course. I will do both immediately. First we will release those two poor creatures who have been suffering in the dungeons since I saw you last. Let us go and get them."

Kei-lin followed the god out of the room and down some steep, dark stairs. Below it was damp and evil-smelling, and one or two rats scurried across the floors out of their way. It did not take long to unlock the dungeon and free poor Heaven-deaf and Earth-mute, who were amazed to see Kei-lin again. The god carried them upstairs, one in each hand, and set them down in the kitchen.

"Eat all you want," he told them. "Nobody needs to look for happiness any more in this palace. We can all enjoy ourselves."

Then he took Kei-lin upstairs to the room where he had surprised them in their midnight search. He opened one of the panels and took out a heavy scroll.

He sat down at the table and read for a long time while Kei-lin perched on a stool, watching and waiting. At last he shook his head doubtfully. "It is not as easy as you might think," he said.

"Why, what is it?" asked Kei-lin anxiously.

"Well, first of all you have to break Chuchuchan's spell over Linza herself. The only way to do this is to make him laugh. This is not an easy thing to do by any means. However, if you succeed in doing this Linza will be free and she can never be touched by him again, as Chuchuchan can never cast a spell over the same person twice.

"However," continued Wen Chang, "although you will be free of Chuchuchan you will still have to deal with the evil spirits and demons that populate his domain. If you can escape those then your way is clear, and the moment Linza steps into the city of Senfu the spell over it will be broken."

"It certainly does not sound very easy," Kei-lin sighed, "but thank you very much all the same. We shall try our best. I am very grateful to you."

"And I to you," cried Wen Chang, "more than you can possibly imagine."

Downstairs Kei-lin met Heaven-deaf and Earth-mute. "I am sorry I was the cause of so much trouble for you," she said to them. But they were beaming from ear to ear. "Trouble!" cried Heaven-deaf when Earth-mute had translated what Kei-lin had said. "We are blessed. We have been hoping for this for thousands of years. What's a couple of days in the dungeon—we will have an eternity of ease."

"I'm glad for you," said Kei-lin, and she gave them each a big hug. "And think about me, and wish for me, and hope for me, won't you?"

"We will, we will dear Kei-lin," cried Heaven-deaf, while Earth-mute nodded his head vigorously, and as Kei-lin and the dragon took off into the heavens she saw two little men waving from the steps of the palace, while the huge god towered behind them.

"And now," Kei-lin said as they sped through the

heavens, "we'll have to rack our brains to think of all the funniest things possible. Can you think of anything funny?"

The dragon didn't answer for a long time. Then he said:

"I can't think of a single funny thing. The more I try to think of something funny, the more depressed I feel."

"It's the same with me," Kei-lin said. A little chill of panic ran through her. "What if we won't be able to make Chuchuchan laugh after all?"

"We can but try," said the dragon, but his voice did not sound too hopeful.

"And what about getting in to see him?" Kei-lin asked. "Do you think we'll be able to do even that?"

"I have thought about that," said the dragon, "and I think I know of a way. As you know, Chuchuchan is one of the most powerful of gods. And unfortunately he is evil too. But there is one thing that Chuchuchan cannot resist, and that is flattery. If we start by flattering him, and continue to do so, he will let us into his house, and even allow us to stay a few days perhaps, during which time we will surely find some way of making him laugh."

They were now flying over massive mountain ranges which Kei-lin knew were the Kun-Lun mountains. On and on flew the dragon, and at last, in the very highest, craggiest, most remote part of the mountains, Kei-lin saw a castle with many curved roofs rising high, one atop another, and flanked by pagodas at each corner.

"The home of Chuchuchan," the dragon called to her, and Kei-lin's heart turned over at the thought of Linza.

The dragon landed in front of a great red gate which had golden cornerpieces and enormous golden handles. He knocked boldly.

The gate slowly opened. The dragon walked through. Beyond the gate was a long, cobbled path leading to the door of the castle. Kei-lin and the dragon walked slowly up the path. Guards and attendants scattered in front of them, for indeed the dragon could look very fierce when he had a mind to. When they came to the foot of the steps leading up to the front door of the castle, the door opened and an extraordinary figure appeared.

He had a bright red cloak which writhed around him as though it were on fire, shooting out tongues and fingers of seeming flame, and a fiery cap which leaped skyward in a scarlet spiral. His eyes were like dark coals and he stared down at them fiercely.

"Who dares to disturb the peace of Chuchuchan?" he roared.

The dragon bowed. "Magnificent sir," said he, "we beg your pardon for disturbing your peace but the way across these mountains is long and we beg hospitality and advice. We know that anyone with such a fine castle would never turn us away."

Chuchuchan stared at the dragon thoughtfully.

"So you like my castle, do you?" he said.

"The finest I've ever seen," the dragon said, and indeed Chuchuchan's castle was very grand.

"Well, well, well," said Chuchuchan, "I don't suppose there would be any harm in letting you in. But who is that miserable little creature you have with you?"

Kei-lin bristled with rage at being called a miserable little creature, but she remembered in time what the dragon had told her, so she bowed very low and said, "Handsome sir, my name is Kei-lin."

"Well, well, well," said Chuchuchan, obviously pleased, "come a little closer and let me look at you. Perhaps you are not as miserable as I first thought." As Kei-lin crept up the great stairs toward him he said, "Actually you're not such a bad-looking child." He held out his hand to Kei-lin. "Come along with me," he said. A great fork of flame shot out of his hand. Kei-lin drew back.

"You're not afraid of me, are you?" he asked, his voice becoming a little angry. Kei-lin looked at him bravely.

"You are very imposing, sir," she said, "it is not so strange that people should be a little afraid."

Her answer seemed to please Chuchuchan. He clapped his hands together and the flames vanished. "Come along," he said. Although flames had appeared to shoot out of his hand, the hand itself was very cold, and chilled Kei-lin right through. She could hear the dragon lumbering up the steps, and she was glad Chuchuchan's castle was so enormous for there was more than enough space for the dragon. Chuchuchan led her into a high-ceilinged entrance hall whose walls were covered with mirrors from end to end. As the mirrors faced each other across the hall, Kei-lin could see her own image whichever way she looked. "Oh," she cried, enchanted, "I've never seen anything like this in my life."

"I'm sure you haven't," said Chuchuchan. He then led them into room after room, each of which was more magnificent than the last. There were rooms with crimson hangings and gold furniture, with silver hangings and finely carved satinwood furniture, chambers on whose walls gorgeous peacocks had been painted with their brilliant tails outspread, and one that was paneled entirely in ivory and jade. Kei-lin was so amazed at all this that she did not need to pretend to flatter the god.

"I suppose you wonder why an ugly old god like me should be living in such a fine castle," he said to her finally.

"You're not old, nor ugly," said Kei-lin dutifully. "You have only to look in the hall of the mirrors and you will see the truth."

The god patted her head approvingly. "You are the kind of child one likes to have around," he said. "How would you like to stop for a little while in my castle?"

"Well," said Kei-lin, pretending not to be too eager, "I don't know. I really should be getting home. My auntie will be worrying about me. And I don't know what the dragon thinks. You see," she added by way of explanation, "the dragon saved me from drowning in a great storm at sea, and we are on our way to my little village."

"Well, I'm sure it won't do you any harm to stay with me for a few days," said the god. "And our friend the dragon has said that he wanted to have a bit of a rest. In fact that's what I want you to do, and of course, I always get what I want." A sudden chill fear went through Kei-lin—what if the god were to enchant them as he had enchanted Linza before they had time to break his spell? She pressed Linza's good-luck bracelet under her sleeve. It was no use worrying about things before they happened, and the first part of their mission was now accomplished—the god actually wanted them to stay in his castle.

"Very well," said Kei-lin, as though she were doing the god a favor, "we will stay for a few days." And she wondered in what part of the vast old castle she would find Linza.

A DUSTY SEARCH

THAT NIGHT they had dinner served in the god's immense dining hall. The most delicious dishes were served, and Kei-lin exclaimed in wonder and pleasure at each new dish, which pleased the god tremendously. The dragon too was generous in his praises, and by the end of the meal the god was in a very good mood. But the good mood did not extend as far as smiling or any laughing. Once or twice Kei-lin had told a funny story about her home life, and although the dragon had guffawed, the god's face remained unchanged. Then the dragon tried, although not too obviously, but the god remained impassive and when Kei-lin laughed too heartily he looked at her disapprovingly and she stopped.

She was given one of the most beautiful rooms in the castle, decorated in pink and gold, and the dragon stationed himself outside her door. In the middle of the night, when the god was asleep, Kei-lin crept out and they talked in low voices.

"I would like to try and find Linza," Kei-lin said. "I want to tell her that we're here and that we're trying our best to break the spell."

"I don't think you should take the chance," the dragon said. "You might be caught, and then the game will be up. She will just have to wait until we break the spell. He must not suspect us."

The next two days were very hard ones for Kei-lin. The god kept her at his side all day, for he was so pleased with her pleasure in everything he showed her, but nothing she said or did brought the slightest glimmer of a smile to his face, and when she laughed at anything he became angry and his eyes started to glow like real coals in a fire.

"He has begun to suspect us," the dragon said. "I'm sure of it. He knows we are trying to make him laugh. I think we are in danger, Kei-lin. I hate to say this, and to frighten you, but I really think we are."

"Well, what shall we do then?" Kei-lin asked. She was near to tears but she knew it was no use crying. She had to think.

"I don't know," the dragon admitted.

"Suppose we try and find Linza and simply carry her away with us," Kei-lin suggested. "It seems impossible to make Chuchuchan laugh. It's the only thing to do."

"Perhaps we might," the dragon agreed, although he was very unwilling.

"Tonight, when the god is asleep, let's try," Kei-lin urged him.

"All right," the dragon said. "We'll try."

That night they waited until they were perfectly certain that everyone in the castle had gone to bed.

They had no idea where to look for Linza, but Kei-lin knew that there was a large portion of the castle to which the god had never taken her. She had asked him what was in that part of the castle, but he had never told her. There was nothing, he had said: it was old and crumbling and rather dangerous, and he had never bothered to keep it up nicely like the parts he had shown her. But Kei-lin was sure that that was the part of the castle in which he kept Linza.

"I'll lead the way," she said. "I'm sure I know where he keeps her."

So, scarcely breathing, and creeping along in their stealthiest manner, the dragon and Kei-lin made their way along the dark passageways of the castle, bent on finding Linza. A bat streaked past them, flying low, and cobwebs stretched their long, sinewy talons after them, and clouds of dust arose but they were determined to search everything.

"My, it's dusty in here," the dragon grumbled, but Kei-lin only said "shshsh." It was when they were feeling their way along a particularly dusty corridor, that the dragon suddenly drew in a great gasp of air and, crying "Look out!" gave a tremendous sneeze.

Now, a dragon's sneeze is no light matter. It was a stupendous explosion. The walls resounded with the echoes, the dust swirled around in mad clouds, and a scattering of plaster fell down around Kei-lin's head.

"Come on," the dragon spluttered, "we'll have to get out of here. They will have heard me." He hurried Kei-lin along the corridor and across another hall. At the end of the hall he stopped again, gasping for breath, and then sneezed again, louder than the first time. The walls literally shook. By now the castle had been aroused. The sounds of the explosions, although they were in the old wing, carried easily on the still, clear night air, and Kei-lin could hear servants and guards running and shouting somewhere beyond them. She and the dragon began to run too, but in their panic they mistook their way and as they burst out of one of the passageways, they found themselves, to their horror, in the very main entrance hall of the castle itself. As they stood there, surrounded by frightened guards and servants, the dragon sneezed again. And again. And again.

And then he hiccupped. It was a vast hiccup, and some of the servants standing nearby giggled. It really was a very funny hiccup. Then he sneezed again. Then he hiccupped. Then he sneezed and hiccupped, sneezed and hiccupped in turn, while more and more of the guards and servants began to laugh. And upon all this, at the top of the stairs, appeared Chuchuchan himself.

He looked down at the dragon and Kei-lin. They were covered with dust and cobwebs. As the dragon looked at Chuchuchan he hiccupped. Next he sneezed. Next he hiccupped three times in a row. And then the impossible happened. Chuchuchan began to laugh.

At first it was a little chuckle, as though he were trying to keep it in with all his might. Gradually it grew into a chortle, and finally Chuchuchan threw back his head and roared with laughter. He laughed and laughed and laughed, so that the castle walls shook with his laughter, just as they had shaken with the dragon's sneezing. And as he laughed the strangest thing began to happen. The castle began to melt away and disappear.

Kei-lin hung on to the dragon's leg and watched in amazement. The walls of the castle were disappearing and the ceiling was dissolving into thin air. Outside the night was over, and the first rays of the sun came pouring in through the windows, but even as they struck the windows these dissolved too, and one by one the servants and the guards faded away before Kei-lin's eyes. And then with one last shriek of laughter Chuchuchan himself rose into the air and vanished, like a soap bubble in a gust of wind. And as the echoes of his last laugh died way, Kei-lin and the dragon found themselves standing alone on a desolate crag.

"But Linza!" cried Kei-lin, "what about Linza? Has she, too, vanished?"

"No, no, I haven't, dear Kei-lin," came a cry from behind them, and swinging around they saw Linza running toward them. She caught Kei-lin in her arms and hugged her tight. "I don't know what

you did," Linza cried, "but you've broken the spell of Chuchuchan, and I'm free. Oh, how glad I am to see you. But tell me, tell me everything."

Of course it was first necessary to introduce the dragon, for although Linza had heard of him, she had never seen him, and then Kei-lin told her everything that had happened, and the two cousins hugged each other joyfully.

"I wish I could say that all's well that ends well," said the dragon, "but of course you know that all has not yet ended, don't you?"

"Oh dear," cried Kei-lin. "I had almost forgotten; I was so happy to have got rid of Chuchuchan, and to see Linza again."

"Why, what's the matter?" asked Linza anxiously.

"Well, as Kei-lin remembers, no doubt," said the dragon, "the God of Literature warned us about the wicked demons and spirits that inhabit this realm of Chuchuchan, and who will probably try to prevent us from leaving. I don't quite know what will happen, and neither did Wen Chang, but we will have to take our chance. There is nothing else to do."

"We will have to fly on the dragon's back," Kei-lin explained to Linza. "It isn't as bad as it looks; in fact it's quite comfortable, once you know how to settle yourself."

Linza wasn't too sure about sitting on the dragon's back and being carried thousands of feet up into the air. She was very nervous about it, but when Kei-lin explained how to hold tightly on to the dragon's scales, and when she had examined them and found them indeed strong and easy to hold to, she became happier about it. The dragon promised not to fly too high or too fast, but first he begged to be allowed to have a little sleep, as he was very tired from the adventures of the night before.

So while the dragon slept Linza and Kei-lin talked endlessly, going over and over again all the events of the past month.

At last, toward evening, the dragon awoke and awakened the girls. He was refreshed and ready for his next long flight. They were all quite desperately hungry by then, and the dragon led them to a ledge where they found some berry bushes, and Kei-lin and Linza made a meal of the berries. The dragon dug up some roots for himself, and although they were very tough and not at all juicy they were better than nothing. Everybody having eaten they were ready to start on their flight.

They flew quite happily for a while, the dragon following the curves of the mountains so that at no time should Linza feel that she was too far off the ground. Linza settled down and began to feel more confident. She found herself enjoying this unusual way of traveling.

It was Kei-lin who first noticed the murmuring.

THE ESCAPE

She listened for a while, thinking it was perhaps the wind playing tricks on her ears. Then she called to the dragon:

"What's that?" she asked.

"What's what?"

"Listen, there's a funny noise in the air." They all listened, and then they all three heard it, a curious humming sound, like that a very tight wire might make when someone strummed on it. Then the humming changed gradually into what sounded like a great number of voices. They seemed very far away, but as the dragon, Kei-lin, and Linza flew on, some of them came closer and they could actually distinguish the words:

"Let's pull her off."

"The one with the pigtail."

"No, the other one."

"Let's pull them both off." And this was accompanied by gales of wicked laughter.

Dusk was falling very fast in the mountains and

when Kei-lin turned to look behind her she saw a livid, writhing cloud following them. It was still quite far away, but Kei-lin knew that it was the army of spirits and demons that Wen Chang had told them about.

Kei-lin called to the dragon, "Can you hear them? I'm scared, oh, I'm so scared. What shall we do?"

"We shall have to fly faster than they can," the dragon replied. "We shall have to keep ahead of them. Hold tight, Linza. I shall have to fly high and fast."

Linza hung on as if for her life, and so indeed it was, and Kei-lin held her so tightly that she almost choked her, while the dragon streaked forward into the swiftly darkening sky. For a while they left the voices behind, and all they could hear was the humming, which in turn faded to a mere murmur, just as Kei-lin had heard it at first. But after a time the murmur grew to a hum again, and soon they began to hear the voices once more.

"They are catching up," Kei-lin cried. "Oh, you must fly faster."

The dragon did not answer for he had to save all his breath for flying, but he too could hear the voices and knew that they were catching up with them. The sun had set completely now, and the stars had appeared.

"Oh, hurry, hurry," Kei-lin cried, but she knew the dragon was doing his best.

Suddenly Kei-lin became aware of something else

flying close beside them. For a moment she thought that it was a demon who had actually caught up with them, but then, to her surprise, she recognized the Goddess of the Northern Star. She was flying as fast as the dragon, borne along on her lotus throne, and she was shouting to them. The wind kept carrying her words away, so she flew faster yet so as to get a little ahead of the dragon. Then Kei-lin heard her.

"They are going to catch up with you," she shouted. "They are the fastest-flying creatures in the heavens, and they want to keep you in this realm of Chuchuchan's. There's only one thing to do, Kei-lin. You must throw the thing you value most between them and yourself. This will delay them and you might have time to get out of their domain."

The thing I value most, Kei-lin thought. Linza's bracelet! I must throw Linza's bracelet between myself and the evil spirits. Oh no, oh no, I can't give up Linza's bracelet.

"Haven't you got anything, Kei-lin?" shouted the Goddess of the Northern Star as she sped beside them.

"Dash them from the highest cliff," Kei-lin heard one of the voices, so much closer that it seemed to be right behind her.

"Yes, I have," she called back to the goddess, but her words were lost in the whistling wind. With a struggle she loosened Linza's bracelet and flung it over her shoulder. Then she dared to glance behind. The bracelet had changed into a huge ring of fire, reaching to the very top of the heavens, and the voices and the humming faded away.

"Don't slacken speed," shouted the goddess. "That will only keep them away for a while. They will get out and then start to catch up again. You must try to get out of their domain before they do that." On and on they flew, and Kei-lin urged the dragon to go faster, although she knew he was flying his very fastest and could do no better. After a while, just as the goddess had said, Kei-lin heard the humming again.

"They are coming again," she shouted, "what shall we do now?"

"Haven't you got anything else?" the goddess cried. "Haven't you got anything else, Kei-lin?"

"No, I haven't," Kei-lin cried, and then she remembered the unicorn's box lying in her pocket. "Oh, no, not that," she wept, but her words were swept away by the pitiless wind, and she knew that she would have to give up the box too.

The voices were coming very close again. "We will throw them both into the deepest dungeon for trying to escape." "We'll keep them there for a thousand years." Kei-lin undid the flap of her pocket and took out the lovely little box the unicorn had given her. "Good-bye," she said softly as she threw it over her shoulder.

"Now come on," called the goddess, "faster than ever." Kei-lin looked behind her, and the unicorn's box had turned into a great mountain of emeralds, piled up to the top of the sky, glowing a bright green in the dark night.

"That will take them a while," called the goddess. "Come on, hurry, hurry."

On and on they flew and still they had not reached the boundary of the domain of Chuchuchan. Once again the humming started.

"They're over the mountain," the goddess cried, "they're catching up again."

"I have nothing else," cried Kei-lin, "nothing precious. Nothing I love. Have you, Linza?"

"No, nothing," Linza answered.

"We're lost," cried Kei-lin, "they're catching up again," for she had glanced behind and the black cloud was almost upon them, and she had caught a glimpse of angry faces and reaching hands and clawing fingers. "Oh, Linza, we are done for," she sobbed.

"The boundary's just beyond that line of hills," screamed the goddess. "Just a few more moments. Oh, hurry, hurry. Kei-lin, haven't you anything else? It's just a few more moments. They're upon us!"

"I have," the dragon shouted suddenly. "The most precious thing in the world to me. And here it goes." And to Kei-lin's horror he gave a great wiggle in mid-air and dropped his tail.

The cloud of spirits was so close that one of them had almost succeeded in grasping Kei-lin's shoulder. The dragon's tail fell between them and the spirits, and immediately an enormous forest of trees grew up behind them, right to the top of the sky.

"We've made it, we've made it," called the Goddess of the Northern Star. "There's the boundary over there, and Senfu is only two miles away."

"But at what a price," cried Keilin, "oh, at what a price!" And she was thinking only of the dragon's tail, for he could not fly properly without his tail and he would never be a real dragon again.

"Oh, how could you do that?" she cried as they slackened speed and dropped earthward. "Oh, that was too much to give away. What will you do now?"

"Something will turn up," said the dragon cheerfully. "You know, I've never really lost it yet. I'll get it back somehow. Now I'll have to concentrate on getting to Senfu, because you know I'm not very good at flying without my tail."

"You have saved our lives," Kei-lin said to the Goddess of the Northern Star, "but I wish it didn't have to be at the expense of the dragon's tail. I don't even care about the other things compared with his tail."

"Well," said the Goddess of the Northern Star, coming very close to Kei-lin and winking at her with one of her three eyes, "we shall see what we can do about that." And by the way she said it Kei-lin felt better, although she couldn't imagine what the goddess could do.

"Look, there's Senfu," cried Linza, and indeed there it was, a silent city bathed in moonlight and locked in the spell of Chuchuchan.

"I shall leave you now," said the Goddess of the Northern Star. "Your mission will be accomplished

the moment Linza sets foot in the city. Good-bye—
and I shall be keeping an eye on you—always."

"Good-bye and thank you," called Kei-lin and
Linza and the dragon. The goddess crossed her
eighteen arms and bowed her head, and then shot
away into the heavens at a great speed.

The dragon put on a last spurt of speed, which
was very difficult for him without his tail, and flew
over the walls of the city, into the city itself. The
moment the dragon set Linza down in the courtyard of her home the whole city started to awake
from its sleep. People sat up, rubbing their eyes and
wondering whatever had come over them. Everyone went on doing exactly what he had been in the
act of doing when the wicked Chuchuchan had
thrown the spell over the city.

Of course there were many cries of fear and
amazement when the people woke up and saw the
dragon, but when they saw that he had brought
Linza back safe and sound and that Kei-lin was
with him, and quite unafraid of him, they lost their
fear. "But what a strange dragon," they whispered
among themselves; "why, he hasn't any tail!"

The sun rose soon after this, and it took a whole
day to recount everything and to rejoice at the
fortunate turn of events. It was toward evening that
a peasant came to the gates of the city, dragging
something in his cart, a very uncommon something
indeed. He said he had no idea what it was but he
had found it on the pathway outside the gates and
felt that someone in the city might know what it

was and might even pay him for it. Everyone went to the gates to see the strange object in the peasant's cart, and Kei-lin and Linza went too, just out of curiosity, and when Kei-lin saw the thing in the cart she gave a great shriek of joy and fell upon it as upon a beloved friend. For it was nothing less than the dragon's tail!

No one had any idea how it could have gotten from the enchanted domain of Chuchuchan to the pathway outside the city, but Kei-lin had a very good idea. That night she went out into the courtyard, long after everyone else was asleep, even the dragon, who was snoring quietly in a corner, and she searched out the North Star among all the other stars.

She stretched out her arms toward it, clasping her hands. "Thank you, dear goddess," she whispered, "thank you very, very much," and surely it was not her fancy that she saw the star winking at her, and that she heard a low laugh wafting past her on the night wind.

ABOUT THE AUTHOR

ELFREIDA READ was born in Russia, where she lived until she was three years old, at which time her family left the country because of the revolution. They moved to Shanghai, China, where Elfreida Read grew up and lived until 1947. Then she and her husband and baby daughter moved to Vancouver, Canada, where they live today. The Reads also have a young son.

Elfreida Read is a versatile author who has received several awards for her poetry, plays, and short stories. She wrote *The Spell of Chuchuchan* because she feels that "many of the deeper meanings in the Chinese myths are as applicable to us today as they were in the days when the myths were first evolved, and it would not harm any of us to get better acquainted with such personages as the Goddess of Mercy, and with the philosophy behind the Yin and the Yang and the ever-present and all-embracing friendliness of the Goddess of the Northern Star."

1   2   3   4   5   71   70   69   68   67